THE SIGIL DETECTIVE
A RIGA HAYWORTH PARANORMAL MYSTERY
KIRSTEN WEISS

misterio press

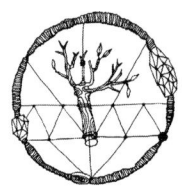

About This Book

Metaphysical detective Riga was never all powerful. But she used to have more magical juice than she does now. Now, she's back to basics… and trapped in a faux-Viking village. But will brains and the basics of magic be enough to bring a murderer to justice?

This Riga Hayworth novelette set during the Halloween season takes place immediately before the events in *The Alchemical Detective*. It was originally published in the *Moons, Magic and Mystery* Anthology in October, 2021.

COPYRIGHT

THIS BOOK IS A work of fiction. Names, characters and incidents are either the product of the author's imagination or are used fictitiously. Any resemblance to actual persons, living or dead, is entirely coincidental.

Copyright ©2022 Kirsten Weiss. All rights reserved, including the right to reproduce this book, or portions thereof, in any form. No part of this text may be reproduced, transmitted, downloaded, decompiled, reverse engineered, or stored in or introduced into any information storage and retrieval system, in any form or by any means, whether electronic or mechanical without the express written permission of the author. The scanning, uploading, and distribution of this book via the Internet or via any other means without permission of the publisher is illegal and punishable by law. Please purchase only authorized electronic editions, and do not participate in or encourage electronic piracy of copyrighted materials.

NO AI TRAINING: Without in any way limiting the author's [and publisher's] exclusive rights under copyright, any use of this publication to "train" generative artificial intelligence (AI) technologies to generate text is expressly prohibited. The author reserves all rights to license uses of this work for generative AI training and development of machine learning language models.

The publisher does not have any control over and does not assume any responsibility for author or third-party websites and their content.

Visit the author website to sign up for updates on upcoming books and fun, free stuff: KirstenWeiss.com

Cover art by Dar Albert.

misterio press / ebook edition September, 2022

ISBN-13: 978-1-944767-82-2

CONTENTS

Chapter 1	1
Chapter 2	10
Chapter 3	16
Chapter 4	21
Chapter 5	26
Chapter 6	34
Chapter 7	36
Chapter 8	40
Chapter 9	43
Chapter 10	50
Chapter 11	54
About The Alchemical Detective	58
More Kirsten Weiss	59
More Riga Hayworth	62
Connect with Kirsten	63
About the Author	64

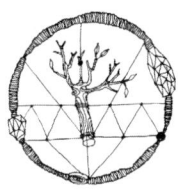

CHAPTER 1

The second thing Riga was sure of was that at least her intuition was still working. She had a rotten feeling about this job.

Behind the high, sleek desk, the security guard stared impassively at his monitor. October sun slanted through the thick, bulletproof windows of the high-tech security hut. Upright, black metal bars, thick and menacing, formed a rampart outside the Odinjörd facility.

The guard's gaze flicked to Riga. She smoothed her auburn hair, brushed a fleck of something off the sleeve of her suede safari jacket.

"What color are your eyes?" he asked.

"Brownish."

"They look more browny-purply. Are those contacts?"

"No," she said. "The purple's an illusion. Just type brown."

"But they look browny-purply."

"Fine. They're browny-purply."

"There's only space for one word." He typed into the computer. Over his shoulder, the ghost of an elderly security guard whispered something in his ear.

And that was the first thing Riga was sure of: she could still see ghosts. Her chest hardened. Spirits and scrying, that's what she'd been reduced to.

That's why she'd come alone, sent her familiar to Macau to "help" Riga's boyfriend who didn't need helping.

She needed to think of something better to call Donovan than "boyfriend." They were too old for it, and "partner" sounded sterile.

The printer hummed.

But thinking of Donovan beat thinking she might be walking into a massive magical disaster. Or thinking about the relief she'd felt when he'd had to go to Macau. If Donovan was there, she could make her mistakes privately here. And she hated herself a little for expecting there *would* be mistakes.

A sliver of motion near the door caught her eye. A gray mouse crouched, shivering. Casually, Riga stretched and opened the door. The mouse darted outside.

The guard slid the small, rectangular printout into a clear plastic Odinjörd lanyard and handed it to her. "Someone will get you shortly."

She read the card. "*Burple?* That's not a color. That's not even a word."

"What do you want me to say? Violet? That's just dumb. Who has violet eyes?"

She sighed, agreeing. "And my name's spelled wrong. I'm *Riga* Hayworth, not Rita Hayworth. Rita was an actress."

The ghost laughed.

"Close enough," the guard said.

The thick glass door behind the guard opened. A weedy young man with glasses and a slight stoop smiled awkwardly at her. "Riga?"

"You must be Jeff."

"Thanks for coming. This way." He stepped outside.

She followed. The door clanged behind them like a prison gate.

They walked down a flagstone path dappled by the shadows of towering redwoods.

"So, I, uh..." Jeff rubbed his wispy beard. "My mom thought you could find something that's missing, since you're a metaphysical detective."

She glanced toward the wooded area and forced a smile. "Tell me about the case."

"I guess my mom told you I was a software engineer? I specialize in enterprise-level software."

She nodded. "Software for companies to...?"

"It doesn't matter. That's not what's missing. What's missing is a sigil app I created. Someone stole it. My mom said you were good at, um, finding things."

She *used* to be. "What's a sigil app?" A sigil was a drawing magically empowered by its creator. It focused the spellcaster's intent. Riga had never needed tech or props before. Maybe she'd need to start.

Jeff's freckled face pinked. "We were talking about what we should do for Halloween—"

"We?"

The trees opened up, and Riga stopped short.

They stood outside a Viking village, complete with a burial mound in the center. Half a dozen sod huts formed a rough circle and faced the grassy mound. Interspersed between and behind them were larger wooden buildings. Two had prow-shaped roofs. One was three-stories tall with curving beams carved into dragon heads.

Riga tried not to gape. She'd known Odinjörd had a Viking-themed logo. She hadn't expected the tech campus to look like Valhalla.

"Lana, Ryan and I," Jeff said. "Living here, working for Odinjörd, we wanted to do something thematic. But there's not exactly a straight line between Vikings and Halloween."

Carrying laptops, two bearded engineers emerged from the tallest building.

"Ryan did some research," Jeff said. "He came up with Viking undead. But with all the zombie first-person-shooter games out there, it seemed derivative. Then Ryan found this witchcraft museum in Iceland filled with magical sigils. So we thought, why not an online sigil creator?" He stopped in front of a hut's arched wooden door and opened it. "This is my place."

She followed him inside the blond-wood house. Pizza boxes lay stacked atop every flat surface, save the wooden desk. Crumbs and crusts and spatters of red sauce decorated the floor. With its stone fireplace, the room would have been cozy if it didn't look like a crime scene. "So you, Lana and Ryan built the app."

"No," he said, "I designed the app. Ryan got bored with it. Lana was busy with her own projects. And then when things went wrong… My mom couldn't stop raving about all the help you gave her with those houses."

And his mother had leaned on Riga to come. It was depressing her biggest clients were realtors looking to de-haunt houses. But it paid the bills. "So you developed an app," she said. "To create sigils."

Riga walked to his desk, where a computer glowed. An Odinjörd logo hung on the wall behind it. Clear plastic dispensers filled with pastel candy stood beside the desk.

"Yeah," he said. "Norse-style sigils, for spell casting." He motioned toward the window, with its carved, wooden shutters.

"I didn't think Odinjörd developed games." Her gaze flicked uneasily to the peaked, beamed ceiling. Silicon Valley was crazy with roof rats. They had to love thatched roofs. And pizza.

"They don't. I made the app for fun. I mean, magic's not real…" He trailed off.

Riga nodded. Spells required human focus and intent. That wouldn't happen if the spell was computer generated. The app couldn't work.

"Do you want anything?" he asked. "Pizza?"

"No, thanks." She studied the Odinjörd logo, a grizzled, one-eyed Odin. Even in his home, Jeff couldn't escape the company propaganda. "So what happened next?"

"I didn't realize everything I created here, even on my own time, belonged to the company. I guess I didn't read the contract very well. But even if I had, why would they want it? Like you said, Odinjörd isn't a game developer."

Riga frowned. "But they do want it? Why?"

He shifted on the wooden chair. "It wasn't so much Odinjörd as the DOD."

Riga blinked, her insides tensing. "The Department of Defense? Is there something special about the programming?"

"Um." He rubbed the back of his neck. "I didn't think so. FYI, the FBI's here too."

Her mouth slackened. "For a sigil-making game?"

"A colleague broke into my room and stole my drive with the app."

She quirked an eyebrow. "No backups?"

"The backups are in the company cloud. But, uh, someone deleted the app file there too."

"And *only* your app file?"

He nodded.

So the hard drive theft *had* likely been related to Jeff's app. "You said one of your colleagues stole it. You caught him?"

"Not exactly. The bartender found her behind the pub." He swallowed jerkily. "She was dead. My hard drive was gone."

Riga froze, her heart jackhammering. "Dead? This is a murder investigation?" She hadn't investigated a murder since her powers had abandoned her. But the FBI and DOD were here too. She *wouldn't* have to investigate the murder. She was just backup to find the stolen app.

Backup only Jeff's mom believed in.

"Yeah," he said. "They're pretty intense."

Stay calm. You're backup. Focus on the app. "Why do you think she stole your drive?" she said evenly. "Maybe she came upon the thief and tried to stop him."

"There are security cameras everywhere on this campus. They caught her on video leaving my hut with the hard drive."

"But they didn't catch her murder?"

"There's a gap between the cameras, a dead zone behind the pub. That's where she was killed."

Convenient. "And you don't have any other backups?"

He adjusted his glasses. "We're not allowed. There's the auto backup in the cloud and the original on my company drive." He motioned to a squarish computer on his desk.

Two dark gray bars struck at angles from the opposite corners of the screen. Riga squinted. It looked a bit like an eyepatch.

"There's a lot of security because of our DOD work." Jeff rose. "Come on. I'll show you where we found the body."

"First, show me how the thief got inside." She stood.

"Um. I didn't lock my hut." He angled his head toward the plain, arched door. "None of us do. There's no point. Everyone here has security clearance, even the bartender. And you saw the security at the gate."

"Everyone's movements are logged in and out? No one who shouldn't have been was on the campus that night?"

"No. FYI, you can stay tonight. I got a hut for you. Unless you solve the crime today." He moved toward the door and grabbed a hover board leaning against the nearby wall.

Riga followed, her eyes narrowing. Jeff was in his twenties—a kid. According to his mother, this was his first "real" job. How had he managed to get her into a DOD investigation and get her living quarters? "Are you sure that won't get you into trouble?"

He stepped onto the hoverboard and glided into the courtyard. "Baldur said you could have one."

She halted. "Baldur Hastings is involved in this?" The mad genius who'd started Odinjörd? The man setting the computer *and* the software industry on fire? The *Forbes Five* Baldur Hastings?

He pivoted the board, traveling in widening circles. "Yeah. When I told him you were a metaphysical detective, he offered a hut."

She took a small step backward and tugged down the hem of her belted jacket. Most people wanted to toss her out when they learned her profession. "That's... generous."

"Baldur thinks out of the box, you know? And the FBI isn't getting anywhere. You sure you don't want anything to eat? Pizza?"

"I'm fine."

"Then this way."

She followed him into the campus's Viking village.

Since moving to Lake Tahoe, she hadn't missed the Silicon Valley crowds or the expense. But she'd missed its smells—the sagebrush, the faint tang of Bay air. And though the massive 101 freeway was only a mile away, she couldn't hear any traffic. Baldur's Viking fantasyland was a world apart.

Two men in dark glasses and dull business suits emerged from a nearby doorway and followed them. She pretended not to notice, but her shoulders tightened.

Jeff nodded toward the largest wooden building, shaped like an upside-down Viking longboat. "That's the communal work space. The pub's over there." He pointed toward a three-story wooden building with angular turrets. A man in red monk's robes sat on a wooden bench beside the front door. "It was modeled after the remains of the Viking temple."

"That's where the body was found?"

He glided toward the pub. "I'll show you."

Jeff led her behind the three-story building and stepped off the hoverboard. He pointed to a grassy spot surrounded by yellow police tape. "There."

She studied the pub's high wooden wall and shuttered windows. Two security cameras extended from the corners of the building. "Okay, she was killed in a blind spot. But her killer must have walked past some camera to get here and leave."

"If he did, they couldn't find him," Jeff said. "Either the killer knew where all Odinjörd's security cameras aimed, or he messed with the videos."

She tilted her head. "With all the tech geniuses on this campus, no one can figure out if videos were tampered with?"

"There aren't that many of us—only the six of us engineers plus Baldur. Then there are the service employees—pub workers, cleaners, restaurant workers, that sort of thing. They're all gone after ten o'clock."

Riga squinted at the pub's steep roof. "This entire campus is for six engineers?"

"Plus Baldur. This isn't Odinjörd's main campus. This campus is for his special projects, and for people who do better working alone."

"People like you." She eyed him. To have been brought into Odinjörd's inner sanctum, Jeff had to have some serious tech chops. "Can I ask what your real project is?"

"No." He flushed. "Sorry. Security."

"And you live here full time."

"I can leave," he said. "There just isn't a lot of reason to. Everything we want is here."

"So there's you, staff, four other engineers, and Baldur."

"Five engineers."

"They've replaced the murdered engineer—what was her name?"

His face fell. "Sarah."

"And they've replaced her already?"

"The Norse campus is highly competitive."

Riga wrinkled her brow. "So competitive you had time to create a sigil app for fun?" She jerked her head toward their two black-suited followers. "Does the DOD know exactly what they're so hot to get back?"

"I think so. One of their engineers tested the app."

"And?"

"It worked."

Riga turned to stare. "What do you mean the app worked?"

"That's the thing." He toed a gopher hole in the long grass. "It, um, works."

It wasn't possible, but she humored him. "How, exactly, does it work?"

"You type in what you want to happen, and then you push a button, and it creates a sigil."

"That's it?"

"Well, the sigil iterates. You know, like those old fractal graphics that used to be used for screen savers."

Riga went cold. "You mean the sigil is constantly evolving? Through time?"

He nodded. "And different shapes correspond to different notes, like in the music of the spheres."

She groaned. He had combined several of the elements of a powerful sigil, a hyper sigil. But it still couldn't work. Not without intent.

He shuffled his feet. "And then what you want, um, happens."

That wasn't *possible*. The spellcaster didn't put any personal energy into the sigil. It couldn't work. But a tiny part of her heart leapt. What if it *was* possible? What if he'd created something truly new?

"How do you know it works?" she asked.

"I tried it." He swallowed. "It works. I tested it."

"Tested it how?"

"I wished for pizza. Five minutes later, I was notified I'd won a year's supply."

Pizza? That explained… Her gaze traveled to the boxes and crusts. "It could be… a coincidence." But Riga didn't believe in them.

"I'd never entered the contest."

There had to be something else going on. "What did the DOD engineer wish for?"

"I didn't ask." He shuddered. "I don't want to know."

CHAPTER 2

"Sure you don't want some pizza?" Jeff asked.

"Yes." Riga stared up at the wooden building. She twined her fingers in the colorful silk scarf tied to her satchel, the scarf Donovan had given her. "I wouldn't mind going inside the pub though."

He brightened. "This way."

Tucking the hoverboard beneath one arm, Jeff led her to the front of the building. Pumpkins lay artfully arranged around its entrance.

The monk on his bench smiled up at her. She nodded a greeting, stepped inside.

The pub's interior was softly lit with hanging sconces and flickering, electric candles. Person-sized Viking runes decorated each wall. Beside them stood clear plastic candy dispensers like the ones in Jeff's hut.

Two bearded engineers sat at tables, wooden steins and laptops before them.

Thunk.

Riga started.

"That's the ax throwing upstairs," Jeff said. "We can try it if you want."

Alcohol and axes. What could go wrong? "No, thanks. How do we get to the second floor?"

"Is this your metaphysical detective?" a man asked from behind her.

The robed monk stood beside another man, tall, blond, and broad shouldered. His eyes were the color of the North Sea in a storm. *Baldur.*

The tech CEO wore a blue knit v-neck shirt over jeans. Both were worth more than she'd earned last month. And probably the month before that too.

"Oh," Jeff stammered. "Yes, Mr.— I mean, Baldur. This is Riga Hayworth."

She nodded. Baldur was the new Steve Jobs, this generation's tech and business genius. His face was ubiquitous, not just in business magazines, but style and fashion as well.

Baldur extended his hand, and she shook it. His grip was pleasantly firm, his smile perfunctory. A golden Norse hammer charm hung on a leather thong around his neck. "I've never met a metaphysical detective," Baldur said in a light, Swedish accent. "And this is Ji." He motioned to the monk.

"Nice to meet you," she said.

The monk bobbed his head.

"My friend Ji has been a lifesaver ever since…" Baldur swallowed.

She'd unearthed that story before coming here as well. Baldur's wife, Agda, had died five years ago of cancer. He'd built this extended campus in her honor, and great things had emerged.

Baldur cleared his throat. "Let's not talk about me. I want to learn about you. What's your process?"

"I keep asking questions until I reach the end," she said.

"How do you know you're at the end?"

"When there's nothing left to ask." Her gaze flicked again to the silent monk. He smiled serenely.

Baldur nodded. "It's not that different from my process, though mine creates rather than deconstructs. Do you think you can find out what happened to Sarah?"

"My focus is to find out what happened to your software." *And how it could actually work.* "That may tell us who killed Sarah." Because this wasn't a murder investigation. Not for her. But she was glad his focus was on the murdered engineer.

"Let's sit." Baldur motioned toward an empty table away from the others.

The four relaxed around the table. The wooden chairs, dragons carved into their backs, were surprisingly comfortable. The monk closed his eyes.

"I understand the Department of Defense is interested in retrieving the app?" Riga edged aside a mini pumpkin, part of a centerpiece of autumn leaves and wooden beer steins.

Baldur nodded. "Everything created on this campus belongs to the DOD. When it comes to outside projects, like Jeff's, the DOD can choose to claim them or not."

"And in this case they chose to claim a sigil-creating toy," Riga said flatly.

Baldur shifted. "Yes. I admit it's strange. But they may have seen other applications in it."

"How did the DOD know about it?" Riga asked.

"Everything input into an Odinjörd computer is automatically saved to the company cloud," Baldur said. "The DOD monitors it. They contacted me almost immediately after the final product was uploaded."

"Why?" she asked.

He spread his broad hands in a helpless gesture. "It's a toy. If the DOD wants it, they can have it. Sorry, Jeff," he said apologetically.

Jeff shrugged. "It's the deal I signed on to," he said, expression unhappy.

"But the app was stolen or deleted before they could take possession?" Riga asked.

Baldur nodded. "If it's in the cloud, the DOD can access and test it, but they can't simply take it. They have to issue a claim, there's a legal filing, and then the file transfers over. But someone deleted the app before that could happen."

"Who could have deleted it from the cloud?" she asked.

"Anyone with access to Jeff's files." Baldur shook his blond head. "Normally, that would only be Jeff and myself."

"Normally?" she asked.

"The DOD and our own team has been checking for signs of an outside hack. So far, we haven't found any. It appears more likely someone deciphered Jeff's password."

"Which changes daily," Jeff said. "There's an automatic encryption key." He pulled a keychain from the pockets of his jeans and showed her a small device attached.

"So someone would have to have taken that encryption key?" she asked.

"I'd swear no one did," Jeff said. "I keep it on me."

"Who else knew about this app?" Riga asked.

"Only Ryan Flemming and Lana," Jeff said. "They've already been questioned by the feds. We're collaborators on another project—"

"Which he can't discuss," Baldur said quickly.

"I assume the DOD searched for the hard drive on campus?" Riga asked.

"Everywhere." Baldur's handsome face tightened. "Jeff told me you worked with his mother?"

"Yes," she said. "Detaching spirits from homes is my bread and butter, followed by finding lost things—"

"Like stolen sigil apps?"

Riga nodded.

"She's been involved in murder investigations too," Jeff said.

Riga stiffened. "That's not—"

"Ah, yes." Baldur nodded. "The racetrack case. I read about that. It convinced me to hire you."

She glanced at Jeff. "I thought Jeff had hired me."

"No one gets on this campus without my say-so," the tech CEO said easily. "Jeff recommended. I hired."

"And the DOD was okay with that?" she asked.

One corner of Baldur's mouth lifted. "I get what I want." He glanced out the window, toward the mound, and his face fell. He said nothing for a long moment, and then he sighed and his storm-tossed gaze met Riga's. "Send *me* your invoice."

"What do *you* think about Jeff's app?" she asked.

"What do I think about it?" Baldur said.

"How does it work?" she asked.

The CEO shook his head. "I didn't get a chance to analyze it. If I had, I'd like to think I'd be able to tell you. But... all I can say is, the DOD wants it."

"So the DOD believes it's useful," she said. "But do you think it works?"

"All I know is that like me, the DOD usually gets what it wants." Baldur rose, his tall form looming over their table, and the monk stood as well. "If you need anything, please let me know."

"Actually," she said, "there are two more things."

Baldur canted his head.

"Where were you the night Sarah was—Sarah stole Jeff's hard drive?"

Baldur's jaw clenched. He crossed his arms. "Home in bed. I'm early to bed and early to rise. Alas, I'm not one of those people who can manage on four hours of sleep a night. The DOD has combed through the videos to prove it."

"And Ji?" She looked to the monk.

"He lives off campus," Baldur said. "He left before the hard drive was stolen that night and didn't return until the next morning."

"The security cameras," Riga said. "Who would have known how to circumvent them?"

Baldur pressed his long fingers on the tabletop. "The security team has been aware of the gaps in the cameras. The team has been removed from campus by the DOD for interrogation."

Riga didn't want to think about what that entailed. "Were you aware of the gaps?"

He folded his arms across his broad chest. "I hire people to manage security so I don't have to."

It wasn't an answer, and her lips flattened.

"The DOD is certain the videos weren't altered," he continued. "And now if you'll excuse us?" He nodded to her, and Baldur and Ji strode from the pub.

"He's pretty amazing," Jeff breathed. "Right?"

Riga raised her brows, and Jeff reddened.

"Okay," he said, "I sound like a fanboy. But he *has* changed the world."

Baldur did have a certain world-bending charisma. But he was no Donovan.

"If you think I've got it bad, you should see..." Jeff's face crumpled.

"See who?" she asked.

He looked up and grimaced. "Sarah. She worshipped the great man."

"And how did Baldur feel about her?"

Jeff's eyes widened. "Baldur and Sarah? No way. He's still got a thing for his dead wife."

She nodded. "Let's go upstairs."

He leapt to his feet and rubbed his hands together. "Right. Ax throwing. Baldur says it's his meditation."

They walked up wooden steps polished to a honey gold and into a room wider than it was long. A single, bearded engineer aimed an ax at a circular target. He took a step and hurled the ax.

It missed the target, thunking into the wall, where it stuck. The engineer cursed and wrenched it free.

Riga cleared her throat. "Those windows we saw—"

"Oh," Jeff said. "Next floor. The hang-out room."

They climbed the steps to the third floor. Animal skins hung on the walls and lined the floors. Groupings of sofas and small tables dotted the room. A candy dispenser lined one wall. Was this part of the Odinjörd strategy? Fueling employees on sugar highs?

Jeff's phone buzzed. He pulled it from the rear pocket of his jeans. "Hey. I gotta take this. Do you mind?"

"Go ahead."

He hurried from the room.

She opened the heavy wooden shutters and peered down. Yellow police tape fluttered beneath the window.

Someone could have climbed down from here using the thick wooden beams, evading the cameras. Getting back up would have been more difficult, especially carrying a computer hard drive. But it was possible.

Heavy footsteps sounded on the stairs behind her, and she turned.

A man in a black business suit filled the door. He was tall. Bulky. Clean shaven. Cheap suit. Her stomach filled with lead. A federal agent.

"Riga Hayworth?" he asked, but it wasn't a question. "We need to talk."

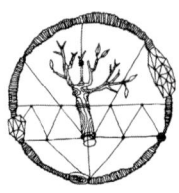

CHAPTER 3

"Sure," Riga said, wary. "Let's—"

"You will not interfere in my investigation." The agent didn't bother to flash his badge.

Riga nodded. "Sounds fair. What exactly *are* you investigating? Just so I'm sure to stay out of your way."

He stared at her for a long moment, his expression impassive. Then he turned on his heel and descended the stairs.

She slumped against the wall. That hadn't been a disaster.

Riga absently filled one hand with candy from the dispenser and closed the shutters. She popped the candy sours into her mouth and descended the stairs to the second floor.

The ax throwing room was empty. Riga sidled inside and picked up an ax. It was lighter than she'd expected. She hefted it. It felt... pretty good. She swung it experimentally.

Riga studied the targets. A low, metal bar ran along the baseboard. The circular targets hung four feet above it. She stepped up to the throwing line, aimed, threw the ax. It spun too low, and she winced. The ax clanged against the metal bar. A blur of metal ricocheted back toward her.

She yelped, ducked.

Thunk.

Shaken, she stood. The ax was embedded in the wall behind her.

Riga looked around. No one had seen her nearly scalp herself, and she exhaled slowly.

Jeff appeared in the door. "Hey, I saw the DOD guy on the stairs. Everything okay?"

She straightened. "Yep."

He frowned at the ax. "Um, you're supposed to throw the ax at *that* wall." He pointed. "Where the targets are?"

"Yeah," she said slowly. "I have no idea why that ax is there. Who's next on our suspect list?"

"Lana Yakamoto." He tore his gaze from the ax. "She knows we're coming to talk to her, but not here. She doesn't like this pub."

"How many pubs are there?"

"Only two." He led her from the three-story building and around the green mound to a low, thatched hut.

Riga paused inside the doorway. This pub looked like the home of a forest witch. A silhouette of Ygdrassil, the world tree, had been painted on one of the blond-wood walls. Bunches of lavender and other drying herbs hung from the rafters. Mini pumpkins lined the windows. Flickering lanterns stood on the tables beside vases of dried flowers. A bearded bartender polished a stein behind the long, wooden bar.

"What *is* it with all the beards?" Riga asked.

"It's a Viking thing." Jeff scratched at his starter beard. "All the guys have them."

A young, pink-haired woman sat on a bench with legs carved into Norse dragons and typed into a laptop. A cup of tea sat at her elbow.

Jeff brightened. "Hey, Lana."

He hurried across the small room and sat opposite the young woman. Riga sat beside him on the sturdy wooden bench.

"Is this her?" Lana frowned.

"Yeah," Jeff said. "This is Riga, Riga Hayworth."

"Hi," Riga said.

The woman leaned forward, her brown eyes blazing with intent. "You've got to get that app back. Can you?"

"I'm pretty good at finding lost things." But Riga shifted uneasily. She *had* been better. In the past, she'd enchanted objects to find their mate, gotten teapots to talk. But that power was gone, and the back of her throat ached.

She *had* to get that magic back. Was that why she'd really taken this case? To prove she wouldn't be forever reduced to the basics of magic, like scrying with a pendulum?

"Tell me about the night Jeff's computer was stolen," Riga said.

"She wasn't involved," Jeff said quickly, and Riga shot him a look.

Lana shook her head. "I don't know anything. I was in my hut."

"Working?" Riga asked. If their computer work was being automatically saved, there'd be records of her activity. An alibi.

"Spell casting," Lana said, and Riga blinked.

"You're a magical practitioner?" Riga asked.

"A techno pagan." She sipped her tea.

Riga nodded. Techno pagans incorporated modern technology into neopagan rituals. She didn't get it, but it seemed to work.

"So I understand the stakes," Lana continued. "Everything has a spirit—cities, roads, cars, computers. The spirit in this app is powerful."

"Are you sure there's a spirt inside it?" Riga asked.

"*Everything* has a spirit." Lana's hands tightened on her mug. "But that's not what's important. What's important, is in the wrong hands, that app would be a disaster."

"Wrong hands," Riga said. "Like the DOD?"

Lana set her mug down hard, slopping tea onto the table. "No one should have that much power, and especially not the government."

"I don't disagree," Riga said. But why did everyone believe this app actually worked? "If it's so powerful, I'm surprised you didn't tell Jeff to delete his program."

"I did, too late. I didn't think it would work. How could it? There's no human energy in it. I thought it was only a toy."

Riga nodded uneasily. The techno pagan knew something about the laws of magic. That made her belief in the app's power even more peculiar. "Did you try it?"

"Not after I saw what Jeff had done." She glared at him. "*Pizza*."

He shrugged, meek. "It was a joke."

Lana's shoulders slumped. "It could have been worse. Imagine if he'd wished for world peace. How would that have come about? An alien invasion that enslaves us all? The rise of a dictator who forces everyone to bend? It's peaceful when no one has any free will. Maybe the spell would turn us all into zombies."

"I think we can agree Jeff made a very bad thing," Riga said. "But there's no spell that could alter reality on that level." At least, not on its own.

She crossed her legs beneath the table. No, you couldn't alter reality like that, not even with a killer app under a full moon when the veil was thin.

But...

Tomorrow was Halloween. Full moon. Thin veil. What *could* the sigil app do under those conditions?

"Who convinced Sarah to steal his hard drive?" Riga asked.

"Why do you think someone convinced her?" Jeff asked.

Riga plucked a sprig of lavender from its vase and rolled it between her fingers. "She went to the exact spot where no one would see her, and someone killed her there. Someone lured her to that spot and stole your hard drive. I suppose it's possible it was all her idea, and she was betrayed—"

"No, it *isn't* possible." Lana shut her laptop. "Sarah was a clever developer, but she didn't come up with a single original idea. She was the person you told your crazy ideas to, and she figured out how to implement. It was amazing what she could pull off," she said, grudging.

"Who do you think was her partner?" Riga asked.

A waiter with a braided beard approached their table. "Can I get you anything?"

"The turmeric tea's good." Lana nodded toward her cup.

"I'll have one," Ryan said eagerly.

"Nothing, thanks," Riga said.

They watched the waiter amble away.

"It had to be Ryan." Lana's upper lip curled. "Sarah had a *huge* crush on him."

And not on Baldur? "And what's Ryan's interest in the app?" Riga glanced at Jeff.

"Ruining Jeff," she said promptly.

"Lana," Jeff said, "he's not—"

"He is." Lana leaned across the table. "He's always been jealous of you. He was top dog wherever he went—at school, on the main campus. And then he came here, and he wasn't anymore, because of you. He hates you."

The door opened, flooding the room with bright, natural light. It closed behind a man in a blue suit.

Riga groaned.

"What is it?" Jeff asked.

"More feds," Riga said. The newcomer had to be with the feds. Aside from the monk, they were the only cleanshaven men on campus.

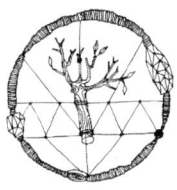

CHAPTER 4

"I'll be back." Riga rose from their bench and crossed the bar.

The agent met her by the bar. The shelves behind it were lined with wooden steins. "Riga Hayworth, I presume?"

She jerked down the hem of her suede jacket. "Yes. And I'm here because Baldur got permission from the government," she said to forestall him. "I'll stay out of your investigation, but we both know I've got my own."

The man smiled. "I'd hope so. Though I expected something more outré from a metaphysical detective. But here you are, interviewing suspects and examining crime scenes. That's *my* gig."

And so was putting suspects at ease, right before the feds pulled the rug out from beneath them. "It's more efficient if I understand the situation," she said.

He lifted a brow. "As every psychic conman knows but won't admit." The agent reached into the inside pocket of his sports jacket and pulled out a card.

She glanced at it. *FBI*.

"You have a solid reputation with several Bay Area police departments," he continued. "Call me if you find anything. I won't complain about you interfering if you point me in the right direction. And I have a feeling we're running out of time."

Her stomach rolled. *Time*. An occultist had once told her that time didn't exist. And yet she wanted to go back to a time when she had all her magic. There *had* to be… She shook her head. "And your colleague with the DOD?"

"He's been looking for a reason to arrest you since you stepped foot inside the compound. When he finds out you've been talking to his suspects, that'll do." He winked and strolled from the pub.

The door closed behind him, and the room darkened.

Riga returned to the table.

"That guy's a jerk," Lana said.

"He beats the DOD dude," Jeff said.

"They both want the same thing." Lana's hands fisted on the wooden table. "They can't have it. That program's too dangerous to exist."

And yet it did. *How?*

They circled the earthen mound and stopped in front of a thatched hut. "Ryan's expecting us." Jeff knocked on its door.

"Enter, and beware," a man shouted from inside.

Jeff shrugged and opened the door. They walked inside.

Blond wood. Peaked, beamed roof. Minus the pizza boxes, the room was the mirror image of Jeff's, with a fireplace on the left, and the desk on the opposite wall.

Something rustled in the thatched roof, and Riga's skin twitched.

Their final suspect, Ryan, turned from his desk. One corner of his mouth curled upward. "The metaphysical detective, I presume."

"That's me." She guessed he'd be over six feet standing. Ryan was handsome, his form lean and muscular, his hair dark. "Mind if I ask you some questions?"

"Depends on the questions," Ryan said.

"Where were you when Jeff's computer was being stolen?"

"Hm." He finger combed his trim, black beard. "If I admit to knowing when his computer was stolen, that would make me a suspect... If I hadn't been asked that question a dozen times by *real* investigators already."

Jeff's face colored. "Ryan—"

"Investigators who don't usually bring their client along for the interrogation." Ryan's tone hardened.

Fair enough. "Would you give us a moment?" Riga asked her client.

Jeff hesitated, then nodded. "Sure." He stepped outside, closing the wooden door behind him.

"Something going on between you and Jeff?" Riga asked the engineer.

Ryan exhaled and leaned back in his chair. "It's complicated."

"Want to uncomplicate it?"

"No," he said shortly.

"So where were you when his hard drive was stolen?" Riga asked.

"I was here," Ryan said, "working."

"On your computer?" She nodded toward the computer and realized the odd lines did turn the screen into an eyepatch: the one-eyed god Odin's. "You'd have a record of keystrokes then? Saved files?"

"They're not recording keystrokes." But a shadow crossed his angular face. "Work gets uploaded automatically every fifteen minutes. It records over the last uploaded file with the same name."

"Then there's no record you were actually putting anything new into that computer." Once she saw the eyepatch, she had a hard time not seeing it, a hard time looking away. It was like gazing into Odin's glowing, empty eye socket.

"No," he said.

"Why do *you* think Jeff's program worked?"

He looked away. "It didn't. It was a trick."

She raised a brow. "The government seems serious about getting it back."

"Who said bureaucrats can't be gullible?"

"And Lana?" She folded her arms. "Is she gullible too?"

"No. She's not." He met her gaze, and she saw that to Ryan, Lana was more than a fellow engineer. He had feelings for the techno pagan.

"Lana seems to think there's something to Jeff's program," she said.

His left hand twitched. "There's nothing to that app. But we never should have encouraged it. Jeff's smart but unstable."

"Unstable?"

He barked a laugh. "He didn't tell you? He's on psych meds. The pressure is intense at Odinjörd. Odds are he destroyed his own computer, deleted his own cloud files. He should see about upping his dose."

Her muscles hardened. No, Jeff *hadn't* told her. Neither had his mother. But that could explain the edge of fear in her voice when she'd roped Riga into this investigation. "Why up his dose now? Is there more going on here than I know about?"

"Probably." He turned back to his computer. "Ask Jeff."

She glanced out the window. Jeff paced at the top of the mound, his head down.

A broad-shouldered man in black strode toward her, and she quick-stepped from the window, her heart pounding. *The DOD investigator.*

He was looking for a reason to arrest her, and he was headed straight for Ryan's hut. She glanced at the bedroom door. No, she still had *some* self-respect.

Riga drew in her energies, muttered a prayer of protection. She visualized herself stepping out of her body and throwing a cloak like a gray blanket over her.

Cloaking spells were tricky. If someone was looking for you, or expected you to be there, the spell could be penetrated. If the DOD agent suspected she was here…

"I need to avoid that investigator," she blurted. "Mind if I use your bedroom window?"

Ryan laughed. "You and Lana…" Rising, he opened the bedroom door with a sardonic bow. "Take your leave, my lady."

She hurried past him, opened the window, and climbed out. Riga told herself she'd try the cloaking spell another time, when the stakes weren't so high.

She rounded the corner of the hut and watched the DOD agent step inside. Ji paced the courtyard. Jeff had vanished.

Riga approached the monk. He looked up and met her gaze.

Something clicked inside her chest, like tumblers turning inside a lock. For a moment, she couldn't breathe.

The red-robed monk stopped in front of her and smiled.

"Hi," she said.

He nodded.

"What do you think of all this?" she asked. "A magical sigil app, a murder…"

The monk smiled, serene.

"Sorry. Have you taken a vow of silence?"

He didn't blink, didn't respond.

"Or do you not understand…?" Riga shook her head. He hadn't been on the campus when the drive had been stolen. She needed to focus on actual suspects. And she needed to admit Jeff might be one of them.

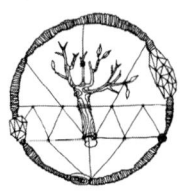

CHAPTER 5

"What?" Jeff said. "Why are you looking at me that way?"

They sat at wooden tables outside the pub. The night air was California warm. Jack-o-lanterns glowed around the pub's closed door.

"I heard you were taking medication that might be affecting your perceptions," she said.

"Ryan." He swore. "They don't affect my perception. They just relax me."

She cocked her head.

"I get obsessed with things, too driven. That's all." He gripped his hands on the table. "I've always had nightmares. I used to sleepwalk. The medication is for anxiety."

"You downplayed Lana's role in the sigil app."

Above his wispy beard, his cheeks reddened. "I guess... yeah."

"How much did she really help with it?" Riga asked.

"She gave me a few ideas. I gave her credit in the software." Jeff exhaled noisily. "But that's gone now." He stared unenthusiastically at the beer stein in front of him. "What are you going to do next?"

"Try to find your app."

"Can you?"

She scraped back her chair on the flagstones and rose. "We'll see."

He saw her to her guest house, which was not, thankfully, thatched, and left her. She walked inside, found the bedroom, and flopped onto the bed.

Riga's phone rang in her satchel, and she excavated it from its depths. *Donovan.*

Her heart lightened. "Hey."

"Hey to you," his voice was a leonine rumble. "Why is your gargoyle outside my window?"

Riga winced. *Whoops.* "She's not exactly *mine*."

"Brigitte's your familiar. Not that I mind, but she destroyed one of the hotel's stone dragons ."

"I asked her to look out for you," she admitted. *Was* he in trouble? He'd gone to buy a casino in Macau, and that crowd could play rough. She shook her head. Donovan knew how to handle himself.

"And the dragon?" he asked.

"She usually has a good reason. You should ask her." Riga rubbed her eyebrow.

"Brigitte thinks I don't know she's here. I'd hate to disabuse her. How are you doing?"

"I've got a case."

"Ah." He paused. "That's why you wouldn't come to Macau."

"That and I hate flying."

He didn't respond.

"I had to do this on my own," she said. "It's like—"

"Throwing yourself into the deep end."

"Yes." The tension in her muscles released. He always understood.

"Good. How's it going?"

"It just started. I'm at Odinjörd."

He whistled. "We use their tech. Should I be worried?"

"About me or your casinos?"

"Both."

"Doubtful." She rolled over on the bed and rested her head on her free arm. "I'm tracking stolen software." A memory of the two of them on his balcony overlooking Lake Tahoe flashed into her mind. The lake had been black, the moon tracing a rippling, mercury path across its surface.

They'd talked like they'd known each other years rather than weeks. She still wasn't sure if their bond was shared trauma or shared adventure. She only knew that it mattered. And that scared her.

"When are you getting back?" And now she *did* sound like a lovesick teen.

"Two days. Should I fly into SFO?"

Yes. "No, you've got your own company to run. This shouldn't take long. And if I do need you, Tahoe's not far."

"Understood." He paused. "You'll get it back, Riga."

And she knew he wasn't talking about the app. "I know," she lied.

They hung up, and Riga unpacked her bag. She laid out her magical tools, meditated, and psychically cleansed her pendulum. She told herself she wasn't stalling. She was just taking extra care with her preparations.

It was midnight when she stepped into the courtyard. The earthen mound drew her. There was something uncanny about that empty space, here on the crowded, high-tech Peninsula.

She walked to the edge of the mound. Flagstones etched with Viking runes surrounded it. Riga climbed the grassy hill and sat crosslegged at the top. She dangled her quartz pendulum between her fingers.

I am looking for the magic of others. Show me.

The pendulum hung straight down.

Asking the right question was key to successful pendulum magic. She'd phrased her request poorly.

Something pale flickered in the corner of her vision. Riga paused, eyes straining. But the mound was empty, aside from herself.

She blew out her breath, refocused on the pendulum. *Direct me to the hard drive with Jeff's sigil app.*

The pendulum didn't budge.

Her hand clenched, and the crystal trembled on its chain. She rolled her shoulders. *Fine. Back to basics, back to ritual.* "I call in my guardians of the light—"

The pale something flickered again at the edge of her awareness. Slowly, Riga turned. A slender woman stood on the mound, her expression bereft.

"I'm Riga. Who—?"

The woman's image faded and vanished.

Another ghost. But they were everywhere, and she couldn't help them all. Riga centered herself. "I call on my guardians, here for my greatest and highest good."

Cold electricity rippled through her, and then a thick longing. Riga swayed. The magic was sweet and repellant. She leaned forward.

Riga shook herself, feeling like a kid after too much Halloween candy. Dark magic had been practiced here, and she gripped her hand to keep from pumping it in the air. She'd suspected a magical practitioner had been involved in the app theft. But now she *knew*, and she could still sense dark magic.

Riga breathed deep, quieting her mind. She visualized white light flowing through the center of her body.

"Riga?" Jeff called from the base of the mound.

Her jaw clenched. She rose.

"I thought that was you." Jeff climbed the small hill. He wore the same casual clothes he had earlier that day. "What are you doing out here?"

"Getting a sense of things. What do you know about this mound?"

"Odinjörd has a brochure on it. There's a story about this Viking who fought a draugr on a burial mound—"

"A draugr?"

"A Viking undead. They're animated corpses, like vampires. They can only be killed by cutting off their heads? Hang around the mounds they were buried in? Though in some legends they're more like corporeal ghosts. But they move more like zombies, dumb and slow."

Could that be the dark magic she was sensing? But if they were like zombies, a draugr wouldn't be behind the stolen program.

"Want to see the brochure?" He pulled out his phone, tapped the screen, and handed it to her.

The mound at Odinjörd is a replica of the burial mounds typical of the period 650-950 CE. These mounds were an important element in Viking ancestor worship. Honoring ancestors inspired the living by remembering the great deeds of the dead. At Odinjörd, we honor the great innovators who came before us, and upon whose shoulders we stand.

She returned the phone.

"Okay," he said. "I guess it's not very informative."

"Is there anything else you can tell me about the mound?"

He jammed his hands in the pockets of his khakis. "There *is* this rumor…"

"What?"

"That Baldur's wife is buried… here. It's not true," he said quickly. "Agda's got a grave in that cemetery off highway 92, overlooking the ocean. But you asked."

But there had been a ghost here. *Agda's?* "Here's what I've got. You developed that sigil app while working on a computer that looks like Odin's eye—"

"Wait. What?"

She twined her fingers in the scarf on her bag. "Screens can act like mirrors, as portals. Normally they're portals to cyberspace, a non-locational space where people can interact with each other and with other things. Like the astral plane."

"Cyberspace isn't magic," he sputtered.

"You told me the sigil is iterative, it changes and grows. That means it's also working through the fourth dimension of time. And it makes music as it changes."

"Well, yeah," he said. "I told you all that."

An owl hooted, and Riga glanced toward the dark spears of redwoods at the edge of the mock village.

"You created a hyper sigil," she said. "The only ingredient missing is magical intent. You'd have to have been working for hours on the app in a trance state—"

Jeff sucked in a breath.

"What?" she asked sharply.

He adjusted his glasses. "I sort of… do work in a trance state. I get caught up in things. Time falls away. But I'm not magic."

But he might be, Riga realized, horrified. "Magical talent usually goes alongside an interest in magic. Your mother is interested enough to hire me repeatedly. And if your mother has some magic, then you may too. The app could work."

Jeff rubbed the back of his head. "The DOD thinks it *does* work."

"*And* you didn't protect yourself with a magic circle." She clawed her hands through her hair. This was a disaster.

"A magic what?" he asked.

"A circle, usually of salt. Magicians pour it around the area where they spell cast. The circle keeps out outside influences." And that logo of Odinjörd had hung right over the computer, influencing his subconscious...

"Of course I don't have a magic circle around my work space. Because magic isn't *real*."

Oh, the irony. Jeff had magic and didn't want or believe in it. And she'd lost it and wanted it back.

Riga glanced up at the fat, gibbous moon. "There'll be a full moon tomorrow," she said, apropos of nothing. *A full moon...* Unease prickled Riga's scalp.

"Look," Jeff said. "None of this matters. What matters is finding my app, if it's still out there."

"Understanding the app will help me find it. The Odinjörd sign on the wall above your desk. Does it come standard in all the rooms?"

"No, Lana got it for me. One day she went crazy at the company gift shop. There was a buy-one-get-one-free deal, so she gave me her extra."

Riga pressed her palm against her stomach. *Odin, god of communications and magic.* Who better to oversee the creation of a magical app? "And you hung it above your computer?"

He scratched his head. "Lana did. Why?"

Her arms dropped to her sides. "Because like a sigil, a magically charged symbol, logos are focused intent as well. They contain all the desires and promises of the organization they represent. Logos *are* sigils, of a sort." And they worked on the people who saw them. People like Jeff.

"But—"

"Did Lana give that sign to you before or after you started working on the sigil app?"

"After. I'd told her about the app, and she told me a magic app needed the god of magic to mentor it along. She thought it was a joke."

"Get rid of it." She tore her gaze from Jeff's hut, glowing with light. "Have you seen Lana this evening?"

"No, is there a problem?"

"Have you ever cast a spell before, Jeff?"

His eyes widened behind their glasses. "What? No. I told you, magic isn't real."

"Not even as a child? Nothing odd ever happened?"

He flushed. "I mean, as a kid, everything seems magic, doesn't it? Imaginary friends, animals and plants—"

She smothered a groan. "Did you talk to plants?"

His color deepened. "It was lame. I thought they could understand me."

She nodded. The app worked. They were screwed.

He removed his glasses and polished them on his t-shirt. "Look, I know the DOD thinks it works, and that pizza thing… But how? How can any of it work?"

"Okay," she said, "imagine we're in a fight. You're stronger and faster than me, more powerful, so you'd win."

"I wouldn't—"

"Now imagine I've got a machete, a tool. Now you can't get near me without losing a limb. That tool makes me more powerful. It enhances my natural abilities."

"Okay," he said slowly.

"Now imagine I've got the sun at my back, and it's in your eyes. All these things together, the tool, working with the natural world, give me the power." She toed the grass. "That said, there *are* martial artists out there who could still take me out barehanded under all those conditions."

She'd once been such a magical martial artist, needing only intent and a word to cast a spell.

Riga coughed. "Now apply that analogy to magic. I'm by myself casting a spell. I can do something, because I've trained and have a natural talent…"

Did she still? "But if I have a tool to support my spellwork, if I'm working with the natural cycles of nature, the full moon, astrology… All those things combined make my spell more powerful. You haven't trained, and you were able to get a year of pizza using that app. That's... impressive. But imagine if someone who knew what they were doing used it. And imagine if they used it in conjunction with nature's cycles."

The moonlight reflected in his glasses.

"I'll keep looking for your missing hard drive," she said.

"The app's probably not even there anymore. It must have been transferred by now."

"Finding the hard drive is where we start."

"Do you want me to come with you?"

"No. Get some rest."

He hesitated, then nodded and plodded down the hill. She waited until he closed the door of his hut behind him.

The courtyard was still and empty, but suddenly she felt claustrophobic, closed in. The high gates around the compound were locked shut. They weren't prisoners, but there was no way to slip out unnoticed.

Her heart thudded dully against her ribs. The sigil app *worked*. Lana was right. In the wrong hands, its influence could be disastrous. And yet Lana had given Jeff that Odinjörd symbol...

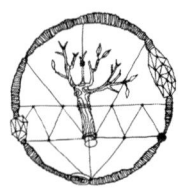

CHAPTER 6

RIGA SAT AT THE top of the mound and stilled her mind. "I call on my guardians, here for my greatest and highest good. I call upon the Divine." She saw white light cascade through her body, and her scalp tingled.

"Direct me to the sigil app."

The pendulum hung, unmoving.

She sighed. When spell casting, you had to incant like you meant it. "Direct me," she boomed. Her voice echoed across the darkened courtyard. A light flicked on inside a hut.

A warm, night breeze blew across the mound, and for a moment, she thought the pendulum wavered. Then, it stilled.

Frustrated, Riga rubbed her thumb against the crystal's sharp point. Had the hard drive been destroyed for good, the app gone, rendering the pendulum useless? Or was the pendulum working, but she couldn't connect with its magic?

Riga whisked her hand along the pendulum's chain, clearing the energy. "Where is Jeff's stolen hard drive?"

The pendulum didn't move. She wanted to cry. She couldn't even do basic—

The crystal trembled, and she held her breath. Heat flowed up her arm. The pendulum swung in widening arcs, north to south.

She clambered to her feet and moved north. An unpleasant, itchy feeling pinged her solar plexus, tugging her backward.

Riga turned south, and the feeling evaporated. She continued in a straight line until she faced the wall of the three-story pub. Riga walked around it. The pendulum reoriented, leading her past the pub.

She moved behind the cluster of longboat-style buildings, past smaller, less decorative wooden huts. The pendulum swung toward a wooded area of towering redwoods. Riga walked into the dark woods.

An acrid scent thickened the air. The pendulum stopped dead.

Riga stopped, listening hard. Pulling a flashlight from her satchel, she scanned the leaf-strewn ground with its amber beam.

No hard drive.

Riga pocketed the light and whisked her hand along the pendulum's chain. "Show me where Jeff's stolen hard drive is. Please," she added.

The acrid smell thickened.

The pendulum bounced twice, then resumed swinging, pointing deeper into the massive trees. Riga followed its motion. Her eyes burned the deeper she went into the small forest. Smoke scalded her throat. The smell was chemical. Choking.

Pulse hammering, she stopped and untied the scarf from the strap of her leather satchel. Riga made a bandana of it, covering her nose and mouth.

The pendulum led her to a clearing. A bonfire burned inside it, flames crackling and snapping around the remains of a hard drive.

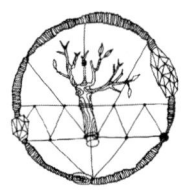

CHAPTER 7

A BRANCH CRACKED, AND Riga started, turned. Smoke billowed, obscuring the clearing. She pressed her scarf against her nose, her stinging eyes straining in the darkness of the small forest.

Her scalp prickled. She wasn't alone. "Jeff?" Riga whispered.

A scuffling sound to her right. She ran toward it as fast as she dared, stumbling over roots, crashing through low bushes. The air cleared, and Riga dropped her hand from her face.

Footsteps thundered ahead of her, a masculine figure weaving through smoke and trees. The footsteps grew faint, the runner pulling away.

And then she was running through the dark on instinct, sensing her quarry still ahead. She'd no intention of catching him, just identifying him. In the past, she could take down a man with her magic. That she couldn't now was infuriating.

They ran. Light from the village streamed through the trees, illuminating his silhouette.

A second, masculine shape loomed out of the darkness. She skidded, tripping over a thick branch.

"FBI," the man barked.

She stumbled into a redwood. "It's me. Riga Hayworth." She raised her hands.

A flashlight clicked on, blinding. She winced, looking away.

The beam lowered. "I smell smoke," the FBI agent said.

"It's the missing computer." She struggled to calm her breathing. "I heard someone. I was—"

"Chasing them?" He shook his head. "Show me."

She led him to the site. The flames had died, the hard drive a melted, smoking ruin. Again she clapped her scarf to her nose.

The agent shook his head and walked to the remains of the hard drive.

Footsteps thudded through the trees.

"This might be a good time for you to leave," the agent said. "I expect those are my rivals. We'll talk more later."

She hesitated, then hurried in the opposite direction. If the DOD found her here, they'd tie up her investigation. And the FBI agent had been right earlier. There was no time to waste.

Riga circled through the woods and returned to the earthen mound. Lights glowed in a few windows, but most of the huts were dark.

She pulled her pendulum from the pocket of her safari jacket. The crystal shook and bounced, but not with magic. Her hands trembled, adrenaline crashing.

Riga walked to one of the huts, raised her hand to bang on the door, paused.

He'd be expecting her to come. He'd seen her too.

She tried the door.

Locked.

Riga hesitated, then raised her hand, palm before the knob. It was a simple enchantment spell. The lock would turn, tumblers falling into their proper places. She'd cast it before many, many times. Chest tight, she closed her eyes. *"Aperta."*

Nothing happened.

Her throat squeezed. *Aperta* had been her first spell, and now it felt as far away as the moon. She grimaced and knocked.

Riga sensed a presence listening behind the arched, wooden door.

"We need to talk," she said in a low voice.

After a moment, the door opened. Ryan Flemming stared down at her, his face pale. "What do you want?"

"I think I can help you."

The sound that emerged from his throat was somewhere between a laugh and a moan.

"What happened tonight?" she asked.

He shook his head. "You can't understand."

"I understand more than you think."

"He told me it worked. It really worked." The young engineer clawed his hands through his hair. "Quantum physics and..." He shook his head. "I thought it was a prank."

"Sarah's death was no prank."

"I *know*. I wanted her to..."

A chill, dark and sweet, shivered through the courtyard. It slithered over Riga's shoulder, and her stomach lurched.

He gulped, his Adam's apple bobbing. Ryan's eyes widened. He darted inside the hut.

Riga raced after him. A door banged. Through the living area, through the bedroom, into a small bathroom.

A door hung open in the bathroom's opposite wall, between a shower and a commode. She raced through into a pumpkin patch, lit by the gibbous moon.

Ryan's angular silhouette loped ahead of her. Dark figures raced toward them, and she slowed, raising her hands.

A man tackled Ryan to the ground.

She kept walking, her hands raised, her stomach twisting. The FBI agent hauled Ryan to his feet and spun him around, snapping on cuffs.

Another male figure jogged through the pumpkins toward her. She tensed, expecting similar treatment.

"What's going on?" Baldur asked, breathing hard.

"Ryan Flemming is under arrest for the theft of DOD property, and the murder of Sarah Tanner," the FBI agent said. His gaze flicked to Riga.

Lana hurried into the pumpkin patch. "What's going on?"

"But it can't be Ryan," Baldur cried.

"We found his security badge beside the hard drive," the agent said.

"How careless." Riga looked up at the moon. Bile swam up her throat. *Too much candy.*

Baldur turned to Ryan. "What have you done?" he asked in a strangled voice.

Ryan straightened. "I deleted the program." An odd expression glazed his face. "I destroyed the hard drive. It's all gone."

Baldur's shoulders dropped. "Then it's over. Thank God."

The FBI agent's mouth curled upward. He shook his head. "You never wanted the DOD to have that program, Baldur."

"What I want doesn't matter," Baldur choked out. "You killed Sarah. Why?" Baldur cried, anguished. "Why Sarah?"

"She knew what the app could do," Ryan said. "I had to."

Baldur covered his face. "I'm sorry for you, Ryan. I'm sorry for what you've done, for what you've become."

The FBI agents led Ryan away. The first agent stopped and looked over his shoulder at Riga. "And I want her out of here, now." They marched off.

"And here I'd thought we'd been friends," she muttered.

"I knew it was Ryan," Lana said. "He was always jealous of Jeff. Always."

Baldur released a shuddering breath. "At least it's over."

Riga nodded. It was too obvious. A security card at the burn site? And there was that sickly sweet feeling, hanging in the autumn air.

The magic was just getting started.

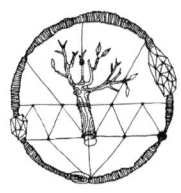

CHAPTER 8

ON THE STREET OUTSIDE the campus walls, Riga leaned against her aging Lincoln and called Jeff.

The engineer answered on the fifth ring. "Yeah?" he asked absently.

"It's Riga. You need to—" *Get out of there, fast.* But it wouldn't matter. Jeff's pizza spell had worked outside the compound. The sigil spell could track him wherever he was. Right now, his best play was innocence.

"The DOD arrested Ryan," she said. "He confessed. But he didn't steal your app. The app made him confess…" How had it worked on Ryan? He loved Lana. He felt guilty about the app. Had that been the app's way into his mind? Guilt, translating into misplaced guilt and then… confession?

And why had the only use the app been put to since it was stolen—as far as Riga could tell—was in getting Ryan to confess? She rubbed her temple. The killer didn't strike her as the kind of person to think small.

So the killer had something else in mind for the sigil app. But why wait?

Jeff coughed. "Riga, what's going on?"

"I'm going to sneak back onto campus. Stay inside, and be ready."

"Sneak? I don't think that's a—"

Riga hung up.

She opened the door to her aging Lincoln and rummaged inside the glove compartment. A pen, a glove, and a granola bar fell from it. Finally, she withdrew a lanyard from a pagan conference she'd attended earlier that month.

She hung the lanyard around her neck. If no one looked too close, they'd hopefully assume it was legit. It was time to jump in the deep end.

Out of sight of the security gate, Riga drew in her energies and whispered a prayer of protection. She visualized throwing a thick, gray cloak over herself.

Riga took a step and stopped, her fists clenching and unclenching. She *thought* she felt the cloak tingling about her aura. Was she imagining the spell working?

She exhaled slowly and strode to the security hut. At its door, she realized her mistake. She'd have to open it to get inside. The guard might not notice her, but he'd notice the door opening, and *then* he'd notice her. She could see the guard through the glass, right there, beside the metal detector.

He turned to watch a TV high up in the corner of the small building.

Mouth dry, she grasped the latch and pulled open the door, slipping inside. Riga gently closed the door. It snicked, the sound rocketing through the small room.

The guard's head whipped toward her.

Another trick to cloaking spells is meeting the gaze of people you encounter. Riga stared at him. Sweat trickled down her neck.

The guard's jaw clenched.

And then he turned back to the TV.

Riga's shoulders sagged. She skirted the metal detector. The next door had a push latch. Slowly, slowly, she pressed it. There was a faint click, and she stilled. When the guard didn't shout, she edged the door open and stepped outside.

The door began to close behind her. Riga whipped around, grabbing it before it could clang into place. She eased it closed.

Keeping to the shadows, Riga walked down the edge of the flagstone path to the village. Men and women in DOD and FBI jackets hurried past.

She reached the back of a thatched hut. Riga leaned forward, peeking around its side. Agents from the FBI and the DOD walked purposefully about the courtyard.

Taking a breath, Riga darted to the rear of a nearby hut. No shouts of alarm greeted her, and the tension in her neck released.

She jogged to the next hut.

No one noticed.

Relaxing marginally, she ran on, darting around the corner of a hut.

And slammed into the muscular figure of the DOD agent.

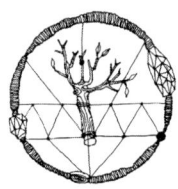

CHAPTER 9

THE DOD AGENT BLINKED, his eyes focusing. He folded his muscular arms. "I thought you were escorted off the campus."

"That's true." He *must* be able to hear her heart pounding. She could barely hear him speak over the noise.

His glance fell to her PaganCon lanyard, and she knew he wasn't fooled. "How did you get in here?"

"The case isn't over." If the DOD arrested her, not even Donovan would be able to get her out. She wouldn't want him to try.

He stared at her for a long moment. Then he turned on his heels and walked away.

Her muscles went limp, her knees wobbling. She braced a hand on the wooden building to steady herself.

Riga dashed the last twenty yards to Jeff's hut and rapped on his rear window.

After a minute or two, he appeared at the glass and slid up the pane. "Riga, what's—"

"Let me in."

Jeff stood back, and she clambered into his bedroom.

His face was white. "Baldur was here," he croaked. "He told me what happened."

"Baldur? Is he still here?"

"No."

"What exactly did he tell you?" she asked.

"That Ryan confessed, and the app is gone."

"Anything else?"

"He asked if I could recreate it."

"And what did you say?" she asked.

"That I could, but I wouldn't."

She shook her head. It wouldn't be good enough. The *possibility* Jeff could recreate it put him at risk. And there was still that sigil program, a weapon… Could it trick a security guard into seeing Jeff as an intruder?

"How are your hacking skills?" she asked.

"I'm no hacker," he said stiffly.

"But could you be?"

"Why would I risk my career?" His nostrils flared. "If I'd had a record, do you think I would be here right now, working on projects for the DOD? For Baldur? I've worked hard to get where I am. I've played by the rules. I'm not jeopardizing my career."

She sat on the edge of his bed. "The app wasn't destroyed."

"But Baldur said—"

"Someone used the app to force Ryan to confess to something he hadn't done. I was there. I saw his face. I felt the magic. The app can manipulate people. I think the killer is waiting for Halloween for his big spell though, when the moon is full and—"

"It *is* Halloween."

"What?"

"Check your watch."

She did. It was past midnight. Halloween. Her stomach spiraled sickeningly.

Jeff grasped the corner of a wooden bureau with dragons carved in its sides. An electronic photo frame with pictures cycling through it wobbled. "So we've lost. Someone took the app off the hard drive, and we have no idea who."

"Of course we know. It was always the obvious answer—the person who had access to your files in the cloud. That's why Sarah was involved. The killer needed a patsy."

"No." Jeff shook his head, because he knew too. "No. That can't be right."

"It's Baldur. You told me Sarah would have done anything for him. Why not steal your computer? It was Baldur's property after all."

"He wouldn't use her like that."

"Wouldn't he? Money and power can warp people. Baldur's been used to getting his way for a long time. He said it himself. He gets what he wants."

Uneasiness wormed in her chest. *I get what I want.* And then Baldur had looked toward that mound...

"He was my mentor." Jeff's fists clenched. "I trusted him. Sarah trusted him. We all did."

"Is his computer connected to the Odinjörd system as well?"

"He'd be crazy to leave anything incriminating there. The DOD has access." The engineer cocked his head. "But..." He glanced again at the photo frame.

She sat on the edge of the bed. "But what?"

"If he's got a private computer, one that's not on our cloud, it's probably connected to Odinjörd's wi-fi."

"And you can get in?"

"Theoretically," he said, grudging.

"If you can find that app in his files, it will prove Baldur was behind it all."

"And if we hand that proof over to the DOD, then what?"

She shifted uncomfortably. What indeed? Lana hadn't been wrong about the harm that app could do in the wrong hands.

"Lana was right," he said. "The government shouldn't have it. Maybe Baldur believed the same." He nodded, leaning closer. "Maybe that's why he took it."

"But he didn't destroy the app. He used it to frame Ryan." She shook her head. "He's got something else planned." And the full moon was rising. "You need to find and destroy the app."

"Do you have any idea how many laws I'd be breaking? It's *DOD* property now. Do you know what they'll do to me?"

"Only if you get caught." And he'd be dead by the end of the week if he did nothing. "Will you get caught?"

He looked down at the dresser. A photo of Ryan and Lana smiling beneath an oak slid into the electronic frame. He sucked in a breath. "No," he said. "I won't."

The next day, Riga clambered out Jeff's rear window and into the sunlight. She adjusted the satchel of Tarot cards and crystals and candles over her shoulder. Pulling a crystal from the bag, Riga oriented using a compass. Riga scuffed a divot in the high grass with her bootheel and dropped the crystal into it. She knelt, sweeping earth over the stone.

A shadow fell across her. Riga looked up.

The monk, Ji, smiled benignly down at her. She hopped to her feet. "Hi again."

He bowed his head.

"I was just setting a protective ward. For the house. Hut. The crystals will form the points on an energetic grid. It's basic magic." *Basics*, she thought, disgusted.

The monk sighed.

"You're right. I *should* focus on moving forward and being the best witch I can be. But how can I? I'm no monk. I don't know how to just live in the present. I've got a past, and it was better—well, the magic was better. *I* was better." Was *that* true?

"I'm seeing someone now," she said.

He didn't reply.

"Donovan's amazing. He's a normal guy—okay, he was never *normal*. He owns casinos. But aside from that, normal. And he went through this mind bending, paranormal… I'd never experienced anything like it. We were in the underworld."

The monk tilted his head.

"I know. It sounds unlikely, but Donovan survived, and he didn't go mad. Most people would have. I came close to—I saw things. Maybe I *am* crazy. Maybe we both are. But I lost my magic, or most of it, and I'm a metaphysical detective. How am I supposed to investigate strange and magical happenings without my magic? I mean, those EVP ghost detectors? Garbage. Fortunately, I can still see ghosts. I just… I just don't know who I am anymore. And yes, I know that sounds like New Age navel gazing, but being a metaphysical detective was my life. And now I don't even know what I'm moving toward. I know that Donovan's a part of it, but then I wonder, maybe he's a part of it because I'm not thinking clearly?"

She paused. "He is pretty amazing though."

Ji smiled.

"Yes, yes, I should be telling Donovan this. But you have no idea how *confident* that man is. I don't know how he'd react if I admitted what a mess I was inside."

The monk's brows lifted.

"I know, you're right. *Not* telling him would be lying. And if he can't accept me for who I am, then we don't have a relationship. But who am I now? How do I move forward? How can I… fight when I've got no real power behind me?"

The monk said nothing.

Riga nodded. She wasn't being fair. Not even an enlightened monk could have all the answers. And why the hell was she babbling to a virtual stranger? It was as if he had his own magic, drawing her out. "Thanks anyway. Good talk though."

Beneath the monk's curious gaze, she planted another crystal and returned through the window.

She sat on the rug in Jeff's living area.

The engineer didn't look up from his computer.

Riga visualized energy from the earth and sky pouring into her. The energies connected in her heart and flooded outward, lighting up the crystal grid she'd built.

"Everything okay?" At his desk, Jeff glanced over his shoulder.

"Let's move that Odinjörd logo." Riga got a chair and took down the sign. She looked around and jammed it beneath a couch cushion.

And then she waited, trying not to stare over Jeff's shoulder as he worked at his computer. She sucked in a sharp breath. "Wait, I thought you said the DOD had access to your computer? Won't they—?"

"They can access the company computer," he said shortly. "This is mine."

"I thought you weren't supposed to have your own computer?"

He shot her an irritated glance.

Someone knocked on his door, and Riga started.

"Get that, will you?" Jeff didn't look up from his laptop.

"I'm not supposed to be here." She glanced at the door.

Jeff sighed. "Then I'll get it." He rose, and Riga backed into his bedroom.

A door opened. She bent her head, listening. There was a masculine laugh, and the door closed.

Riga returned to the living area. Jeff set a pizza box on a long, wooden table and grabbed a slice. His expression turned sheepish. "Well, you can't go out for lunch," he said. "I had to order in."

And Riga needed something other than candy to eat. She glanced guiltily at Jeff's depleted dispensers.

Riga walked to the table and reached for a slice. Her skin prickled. The protective ward she'd set trembled, its magical energies skittering through her veins. She stiffened.

"Don't you like pepperoni?" he asked.

"Pepperoni's fine. Keep working on that hack." She sat cross-legged on a throw rug beside the couch.

Riga pressed her fingertips to the rug and closed her eyes. Pushing her aura outward, she felt for the protective grid. It was still there, but something was pushing on it, testing for a way through.

She returned to her visualization. Cool blue energy from above. Hot earth energy from below. The grid lines glowed, blinding even through her closed eyes. And then they faded a bit, became more bearable.

Warmth spread through her body, and she nodded, satisfied. Riga pushed her aura outward again. The app spell was still trying to find a way in, but it seemed farther away. Weaker.

An hour passed. She stood and stretched.

Jeff stared intently at his screen, his fingers flying across the keyboard.

The hair rose on Riga's neck, and the grid quivered beneath another attack. Jeff's chair creaked.

She sat and poured more energy into the grid. A bead of sweat trickled down her neck. Her elbows pressed into her sides. Her protective grid was weakening.

Jeff rose. "I need a break." He moved toward the door. "I'm going to get a smoothie."

She struggled to her feet. "Don't go outside."

"Why not?" He pulled back a curtain. "There are still a few agents out there and a ton of Vikings." He let the curtain drop.

"Vikings?" she asked.

"Halloween. There's a party on the main campus later. Everyone's going, Lana, everyone. Maybe we could talk to the other engineers there. Maybe they saw—"

"You can't go anywhere," she said quietly. "You're a loose end, and Baldur has your sigil app."

"But I—" Jeff glanced at the door. "What if I can't find the app?" He motioned toward his laptop.

"You'll find it, because it's out there, and it's active now. The program is running."

"How can you tell?"

Riga smiled grimly, her palms tingling. "I can tell." And *that* was more than basic magic. She *wasn't* a basic witch. She wasn't what she had been either, but she was something.

"Whatever." Jeff sat and returned to his keyboard.

Her protective grid shook, setting her nerve endings on fire, and Riga winced. She sat on the rug and focused.

The attacks came in waves. The sun lowered in the sky. The time between the magical assaults grew shorter. And the moon rose.

"How's it going?" she asked between gritted teeth.

"I think I'm getting there."

"How much longer?"

"It's hard to tell. Not much."

A blow rocked her grid, ringing her nerves like a bell, and she grunted. "Good."

Rising, Riga walked to the door and cracked it open.

It was dark, the courtyard deserted. Jack o'lanterns glowed from windows and doorways. Beneath the full moon, a green glow lit the top of the mound.

CHAPTER 10

"Jeff?" Riga asked, gaze fixed on the burial mound.

"Yeah," he said without looking up.

"Hack like your life depends on it."

He glanced up, grinning. "That's a good—" His face went slack. "Oh. You mean it."

"Where *is* everyone?" she muttered.

"Halloween. They're at the main campus."

She bit her bottom lip. Why hadn't that strange glow attracted security?

Jeff stood and peered through the curtains. "Cool light show."

Security must think the light was a Halloween stunt. Maybe Baldur had even warned them about it.

"I'll be back." *I hope.* "Stay inside."

She walked outside, carefully shutting the door behind her. The moon rose, fat and full above the mound, and in its light stood the silhouette of a man, his arms raised.

Baldur. His hands made complicated patterns, the hemlock light shifting in time to his movements.

Neck bent, she trudged forward. She knew what he was trying to do now. He hadn't forgotten his lost love. And the rumor was true.

But his practiced movements… This spell was more than the app. Baldur was conducting a formal ritual. Her hands clenched. She'd never entered a magical battle with so little magic of her own before.

She scanned her memory of other fights, searching for a trick she could leverage. In the past, all she'd needed was intent and a word to levitate objects like missiles, to enchant vines to coil and choke, to call...

Her nostrils flared, her jaw hardening. "Screw the past." The monk was right. She had to fight with what she had today.

Riga strode across the empty courtyard. Green lightning leapt at the top of the mound, and she winced, shielding her eyes.

She stepped onto the mound. An emptiness, cool as the moon, filled her. The full moon, bringing spells to fruition. And now its natural cycle was working with the app, making it more powerful.

Riga climbed toward the top, green lightning flashing around her. Cold power thickened the air until she thought she might drown. "Baldur!"

He raised his hand to the moon. Green light cast eerie shadows across his face. "The moon is full and the veil is thin, Riga. You may have blocked the app from taking care of Jeff but it's working with the elements tonight."

She hesitated. Jeff had combined tech and old magic in his app. And now Baldur was leveraging that app with ritual, the full moon, and the seasonal between-time. How powerful *was* it tonight?

Baldur pointed to a patch of bare soil. Rivulets of earth streamed from it.

Her chest grew heavy, tightening. *Agda.* "No," she said quietly. "You didn't. A resurrection spell?"

"We can go back." He laughed brokenly. "Agda."

"Agda's been dead five years," she said, half-pitying. The other half remembered Ryan, in jail, and Sarah, dead. "What do you think you're bringing back?"

"Agda." He moaned. "It will work. With the app and the moon and the thinning of the veil, it will work."

A clawlike hand burst from the earth. It was a horror film made real, and Riga yipped a hysterical laugh.

A flash of green struck the ground near her foot, raising the hair on her head. "It won't work the way you think it will. It never does. She won't be *right*."

His eyes glittered with madness. "It's a new era, Riga. We know so much more than our ancestors. They failed. I'll succeed."

Her spine bowed. Baldur was lost, mad, but she *would* save Jeff. A tattered arm broke through the soil. "You've won. Now stop your attack on Jeff."

"Stop it? You mean he's not dead yet?" His brow wrinkled. "But the app—"

"Magic has rules. Not even that app is unstoppable." But between the app and the moon and Halloween, it was pretty damn close. How was she supposed to fight this Franken-magic?

She sucked in a breath. But it wasn't only the app or even the moon. He was using classical ritual, and rituals could be disrupted. And the mound was circular, a ring…

Riga turned on her flashlight and searched for Baldur's magic circle. The emerald flashes dizzied her. If she could break that before the spell completed, she might have a chance.

Riga moved down the mound, scanning the grass. There *had* to be a protective container for his spell. If not of salt, then… She hissed. *The flagstone runes at the mound's base.*

She skidded down the hillside.

"You're too late," he screamed. "Agda!"

Riga reached the base and found a flagstone with a rune. This was more than a protective circle. The runes were part of his spell.

Kneeling, she clawed at the earth around the flat stone. A nail broke. She snarled at the sharp stab of pain.

Riga pried the stone free, and tossed it away. Magical energies exploded behind her, Baldur's ritual shattering. The shock wave threw her forward. She flung out her hands. They struck the flagstones, palms burning.

"Agda!"

She staggered to her feet. Two figures wavered at the top of the mound, one standing, one kneeling.

"Riga," Jeff shouted. "I found the app. I stopped it… What *is* that?" He pointed toward the top of the mound.

The kneeling figure, lithe and feminine, lurched to its feet. Agda reached a tremulous hand toward her husband, caressing his face. Her other hand came up, and Baldur's form jerked.

Riga took a step backward. "Well. Damn." Draugrs *were* real. Draugrs, vampires… "This won't end well," she muttered.

Agda lifted her husband off his feet and shook him like an angry child would a doll.

Riga turned, sprinting toward the pub. "Jeff, the pub."

Jeff caught up with her at its door. "What's in the pub?"

She tugged on it. *Locked.* "We need to get inside."

He zipped his lanyard forward on its line and waved it over an electronic lock. The door clicked open. "Are we hiding?"

"We're arming."

"What?" Jeff squawked.

Riga took the stairs two at a time to the ax-throwing room. Jeff's footsteps pounded up the steps behind her. Small throwing axes lined a wooden rack.

Ignoring them, she grabbed a throwing ax off the wall.

She handed Jeff an ax, took one for herself, and raced downstairs.

"You said draugrs are like vampires, right?" Riga panted.

"Why? What do draugrs…? No. No way. You're not saying that thing on the mound's—"

"It is." Riga grasped the axe with two hands. She might not have her old magic, but she had an ax. "Let's hope you remembered the story right."

CHAPTER 11

The full moon sank toward the western hills. Riga sat at the base of the mound, her hands limp on her knees. Jeff lay collapsed beside her.

"That wasn't real," Jeff panted. "It couldn't have been real."

"We should go inside," Riga said.

Engineers would begin returning from the Halloween party soon. The moon would sink. The sun would rise. And a scattering of frail bones would be found—all that was left of the draugr. Agda.

Riga hadn't been smooth with the axe. Fortunately, the draugr hadn't seemed to know much about ax fights either.

"We *didn't* just decapitate a skeleton-zombie," Jeff said. "That was a Halloween trick. Right?"

"Jeff, you must know by now there's real magic in this world. You created a magical app that worked."

"Someone slipped magic mushrooms into my kombucha. Yeah. That's it."

"You couldn't have created that sigil app if you didn't have some magic in you. We should talk about this. There's training—"

"No," he said shortly. "No."

A chill autumn breeze scattered desiccated leaves across the courtyard.

Jeff lowered his head. "Is he dead?"

Riga nudged Baldur with her booted foot, and the CEO groaned. "He'll live."

"But what *happened*?" Jeff asked, plaintive.

Riga shot him an irritated look. She had splinters in her hands, draugr muck on her clothing, and her arms and shoulders ached.

But the attack on Jeff had ended. The only magic she felt now was the magic of the cool, October air. No, November, now. Time marched on. It was past midnight. Halloween was over.

"That… thing was really his wife?" Jeff asked.

"Baldur thought he could go back. You said you stopped the app. You deleted it?"

Jeff grimaced. "I—no. I chickened out. The DOD—"

"You are going to delete that app, Jeff. But first, I think it's got one more spell in it. Maybe two."

The egg sat unmoving on Riga's linoleum counter.

She stared at it, her eyes narrowed in concentration. Riga still had some magic. Maybe she couldn't go back to what she was, but she could be something else. Something new.

"You are not concentrating," Brigitte said, her voice a French-accented Lauren Bacall. The gargoyle's stone claws tensed, gouging the cheap countertop.

"And you're not helping."

"You are simply annoyed that I was of great assistance to Monsieur Mosse, while *you* played detective."

Riga straightened. "Thanks for keeping him safe."

"Faugh." Brigitte sniffed. "*Dragons.*"

Someone knocked on her door, and Riga straightened. The gargoyle stiffened, looking no more nor less than a small, stone statue.

Riga went to the door, opened it.

The DOD agent stood on her porch, his footprints deep in the snow. "Can I come in?"

"You'd better." She stepped aside. "We're letting all the heat out."

He looked around the cabin, his lip curling. "Metaphysical detecting doesn't pay much, does it?"

"Baldur's not paying me."

"Not in jail, he's not. He confessed to everything, *and* to blackmailing that Ryan kid into a false confession. Funny thing, the justice department decided not to prosecute the kid for lying under oath and interfering in an investigation."

"How out of character," Riga said.

"Yeah." He stared, expression hard. "It's almost as if they were under a spell or something," he said slowly.

Riga nodded. "But we all know there's no such thing as magic. And since that sigil app was destroyed when Baldur fried his own computer... Did the DOD have any luck retrieving it?" she asked, knowing they hadn't.

His eyes narrowed. "It's a good thing I think you're just a con artist, and not someone who'd tamper with evidence or DOD property."

"Is that why you came?"

"I came to make sure there weren't any spare sigil apps on your computer." He strode to the card table and grabbed her laptop. "I'll have to take this. And your phone."

She nodded to the flip phone on the counter.

"A flip..." His lip curled. "Useless. Never mind." He strode from the cabin, her laptop under one arm.

The flip phone in question rang. She checked the number. *Donovan*. Her lips curved. Whatever had happened in the past, whatever her magic had become, she'd move forward. And she wouldn't be alone.

Author's Note:

The Sigil Detective takes place immediately before book 1 in the Riga Hayworth series, <u>The Alchemical Detective</u>. Jeff is a recurring character, and I wanted to give him some back story. And yes, sigil apps are a thing.

Sign up for my newsletter for exclusive short stories and more: <u>KirstenWeiss.com</u>.

This metaphysical detective has a murder to solve. But will a devilishly handsome casino owner get in the way?

There's a storm on the horizon. Middle-aged detective Riga's lost her magic and has come to Lake Tahoe for a fresh start and to spend quality time with her new love. But life for a metaphysical detective is never that simple.

Someone's killing psychics in Lake Tahoe, and the police think Riga may be connected to the murders. The best way to prove her innocence? Catch the killer herself... if she can escape the monster-hunting "reality" show she's committed to for long enough. And as the killer circles closer, she may become his next target...

If you love talking gargoyles, smart mysteries, and mature heroines with complicated lives, you'll love this midlife mystery series. Pick up this page-turning paranormal women's fiction today! Because this complicated, Gen-X detective isn't like the others... Start reading The Alchemical Detective now!

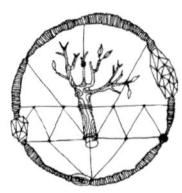

About the Alchemical Detective

THIS METAPHYSICAL DETECTIVE HAS a murder to solve. But will a devilishly handsome casino owner get in the way?

There's a storm on the horizon. Middle-aged detective Riga's lost her magic and has come to Lake Tahoe for a fresh start and to spend quality time with her new love. But life for a metaphysical detective is never that simple.

Someone's killing psychics in Lake Tahoe, and the police think Riga may be connected to the murders. The best way to prove her innocence? Catch the killer herself… if she can escape the monster-hunting "reality" show she's committed to for long enough. And as the killer circles closer, she may become his next target…

If you love talking gargoyles, smart mysteries, and mature heroines with complicated lives, you'll love this midlife mystery series. Pick up this page-turning paranormal women's fiction today! Because this complicated, Gen-X detective isn't like the others… Start reading The Alchemical Detective now!

MORE KIRSTEN WEISS

THE DOYLE WITCH MYSTERIES

In a mountain town where magic lies hidden in its foundations and forests, three witchy sisters must master their powers and shatter a curse before it destroys them and the home they love.

This thrilling witch mystery series is perfect for fans of Annabel Chase, Adele Abbot, and Amanda Lee. If you love stories rich with packed with magic, mystery, and murder, you'll love the Witches of Doyle. Follow the magic with the Doyle Witch trilogy, starting with book 1, *Bound*.

The Mystery School Series

The Doyle Witches have created a mystery school, and a woman starting over becomes a student of magic and murder...

This metaphysical mystery series is perfect for readers who love a good page-turner as well as the deeper questions that accompany life's transitions. These empowering books come with their own oracle app, the UnTarot, plus downloadable mystery school worksheets. The Doyle Witch magic continues, starting with book 1, *Legacy of the Witch*.

The Perfectly Proper Paranormal Museum Mysteries

When highflying Maddie Kosloski is railroaded into managing her small-town's paranormal museum, she tells herself it's only temporary... until a corpse in the museum embroils her in murders past and present.

If you love quirky characters and cats with attitude, you'll love this laugh-out-loud cozy mystery series with a light paranormal twist. It's perfect for fans of Jana DeLeon, Laura Childs, and Juliet Blackwell. Start with book 1, *The Perfectly Proper Paranormal Museum*, and experience these charming wine-country whodunits today.

The Tea & Tarot Cozy Mysteries

Welcome to Beanblossom's Tea and Tarot, where each and every cozy mystery brews up hilarious trouble.

Abigail Beanblossom's dream of owning a tearoom is about to come true. She's got the lease, the start-up funds, and the recipes. But Abigail's out of a tearoom and into hot water when her realtor turns out to be a conman… and then turns up dead.

Take a whimsical journey with Abigail and her partner Hyperion through the seaside town of San Borromeo (patron saint of heartburn sufferers). And be sure to check out the easy tearoom recipes in the back of each book! Start the adventure with book 1, *Steeped in Murder*.

The Wits' End Cozy Mysteries

Cozy mysteries that are out of this world…

Running the best little UFO-themed B&B in the Sierras takes organization, breakfasting chops, and a talent for turning up trouble.

The truth is out there… Way out there in these hilarious whodunits. Start the series and beam up book 1, *At Wits' End*, today!

Pie Town Cozy Mysteries

When Val followed her fiancé to coastal San Nicholas, she had ambitions of starting a new life and a pie shop. One broken engagement later, at least her dream of opening a pie shop has come true…. Until one of her regulars keels over at the counter.

Welcome to Pie Town, where Val and pie-crust specialist Charlene are baking up hilarious trouble. Start this laugh-out-loud cozy mystery series with book 1, *The Quiche and the Dead*.

A Big Murder Mystery Series

Small Town. Big Murder.

The number one secret to my success as a bodyguard? Staying under the radar. But when a wildly public disaster blew up my career and reputation, it turned my perfect, solitary life upside down.

I thought my tiny hometown of Nowhere would be the ideal out-of-the-way refuge to wait out the media storm.

It wasn't.

My little brother had moved into a treehouse. The obscure mountain town had decided to attract tourists with the world's largest collection of big things... Yes, Nowhere now has the world's largest pizza cutter. And lawn flamingo. And ball of yarn...

And then I stumbled over a dead body.

All the evidence points to my brother being the bad guy. I may have been out of his life for a while—okay, five years—but I know he's no killer. Can I clear my brother before he becomes Nowhere's next Big Fatality?

A fast-paced and funny cozy mystery series, start with Big Shot.

The Riga Hayworth Paranormal Mysteries

Her gargoyle's got an attitude.

Her magic's on the blink.

Alchemy might be the cure... if Riga can survive long enough to puzzle out its mysteries.

All Riga wants is to solve her own personal mystery—how to rebuild her magical life. But her new talent for unearthing murder keeps getting in the way...

If you're looking for a magical page-turner with a complicated, 40-something heroine, read the paranormal mystery series that fans of Patricia Briggs and Ilona Andrews call AMAZING! Start your next adventure with book 1, *The Alchemical Detective*.

Sensibility Grey Steampunk Suspense

California Territory, 1848.

Steam-powered technology is still in its infancy.

Gold has been discovered, emptying the village of San Francisco of its male population.

And newly arrived immigrant, Englishwoman Sensibility Grey, is alone.

The territory may hold more dangers than Sensibility can manage. Pursued by government agents and a secret society, Sensibility must decipher her father's clockwork secrets, before time runs out.

If you love over-the-top characters, twisty mysteries, and complicated heroines, you'll love the Sensibility Grey series of steampunk suspense. Start this steampunk adventure with book 1, *Steam and Sensibility*.

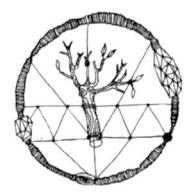

More Riga Hayworth

Prequels
The Metaphysical Detective
The Sigil Detective

Books in Order
The Alchemical Detective
The Shamanic Detective
The Infernal Detective
The Elemental Detective
The Hoodoo Detective
The Hermetic Detective
Unbound

Short Stories
The Gargoyle Chronicles

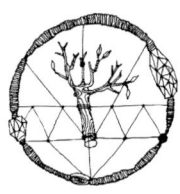

CONNECT WITH KIRSTEN

Sign up for my newsletter and get a special digital prize pack for joining, including an exclusive Tea & Tarot novella, *Fortune Favors the Grave*.
https://kirstenweiss.com
Or maybe you'd like to chat with other whimsical mystery fans? Come join Kirsten's reader page on Facebook:
https://www.facebook.com/kirsten.weiss
Or… sign up for my read and review team on Booksprout:
https://booksprout.co/author/8142/kirsten-weiss

ABOUT THE AUTHOR

I BELIEVE IN FREE-WILL, and that we all can make a difference. I believe that beauty blossoms in the conscious life, particularly with friends, family, and strangers. I believe that genre fiction has become generic, and it doesn't have to be.

My current focus is my new Mystery School series, starting with *Legacy of the Witch*. Traditionally, women's fiction refers to fiction where a woman—usually in her midlife—is going through some sort of dramatic change. A lot of us do go through big transitions in midlife. We get divorced or remarried. The kids leave the nest. Our bodies change. The midlife crisis is real—though it manifests in different ways—as we look back on where we've been, where we're going, and the time we have left.

Now in my mid-fifties, I've spent more time thinking about the big "meaning of life" issues. It seemed like approaching those issues through witch fiction, and through a fictional mystery school, would be a fun and a useful way for me to work out some of these ideas in my own head—about change and letting go, faith and fear, and love and longing.

After growing up on a diet of Nancy Drew, Sherlock Holmes, and Agatha Christie, I've published over 60 mysteries—from cozies to supernatural suspense, as well as an experimental fiction book on Tarot. Spending over 20 years working overseas in international development, I learned that perception is not reality, and things are often not what they seem—for better or worse.

There isn't a winter holiday or a type of chocolate I don't love, and some of my best friends are fictional.

Sign up for my **newsletter** for exclusive stories and book updates. I also have a read-and-review tea via **Booksprout** and I'm looking for honest and thoughtful reviews! If you're interested, download the **Booksprout app**, follow me on Booksprout, and opt-in for email notifications.

bookbub.com/profile/kirsten-weiss

goodreads.com/author/show/5346143.Kirsten_Weiss

facebook.com/kirsten.weiss

instagram.com/kirstenweissauthor/

youtube.com/@KirstenWeiss-Writer?sub_confirmation=1

Manufactured by Amazon.ca
Acheson, AB